For my children with all my love.

Bloomsbury Publishing, London, Oxford, New York, New Delhi and Sydney

First published in Great Britain in 2016 by Bloomsbury Publishing Plc
50 Bedford Square, London, WC1B 3DP

Text & illustrations copyright © Debi Gliori 2016

The moral right of the author/illustrator has been asserted

A CIP catalogue record for this book is available from the British Library

ISBN 978 1 4088 7273 4

1 3 5 7 9 10 8 6 4 2

Printed in China by C & C Offset Printing Co Ltd, Shenzhen, Guangdong

www.bloomsbury.com
www.debiglioribooks.com

All papers used by Bloomsbury Publishing are natural, recyclable products
made from wood grown in well-managed forests.
The manufacturing processes conform to the environmental regulations of the country of origin

BLOOMSBURY is a registered trademark of Bloomsbury Publishing Plc

Goodnight World

Debi Gliori

BLOOMSBURY

LONDON OXFORD NEW YORK NEW DELHI SYDNEY

Goodnight planet,
goodnight world.
Peaceful clouds
around Earth curled.

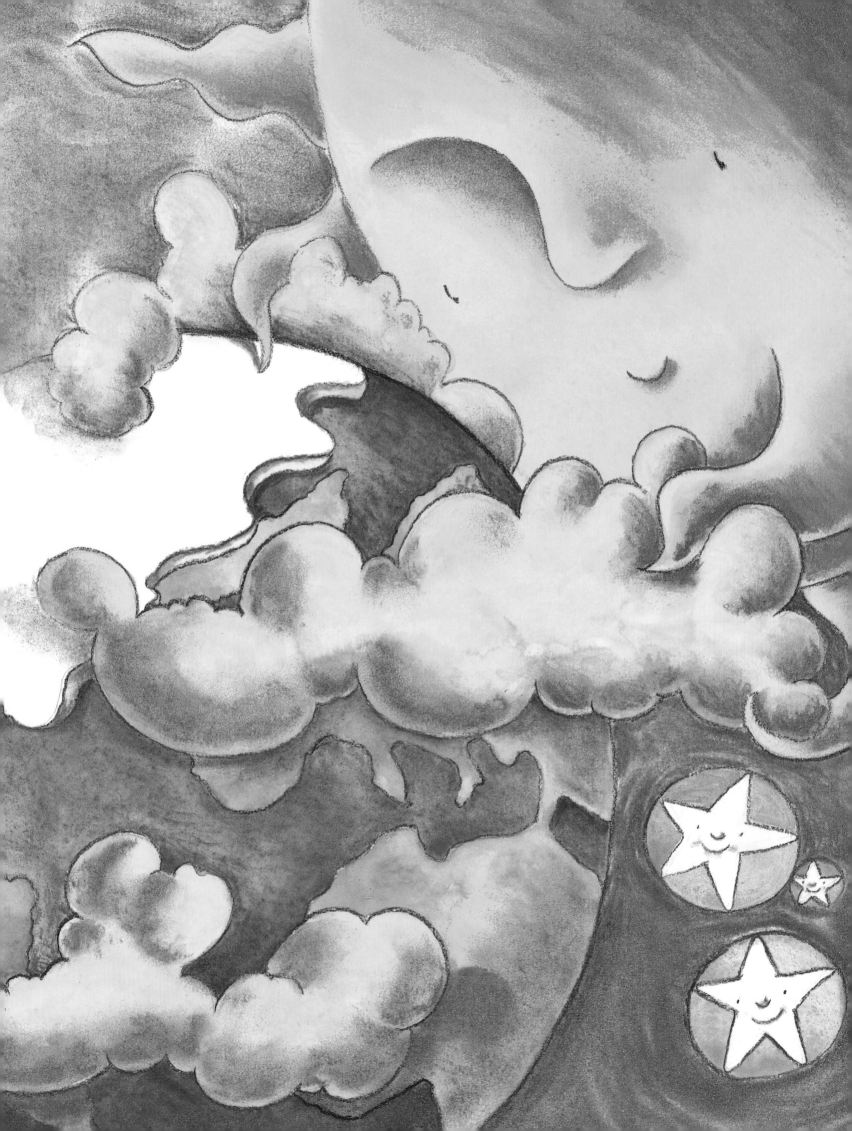

Goodnight ice and goodnight snow.

Goodnight lights above, a-glow.

Goodnight oceans
deep and wide,

rocking ships
upon the tide.

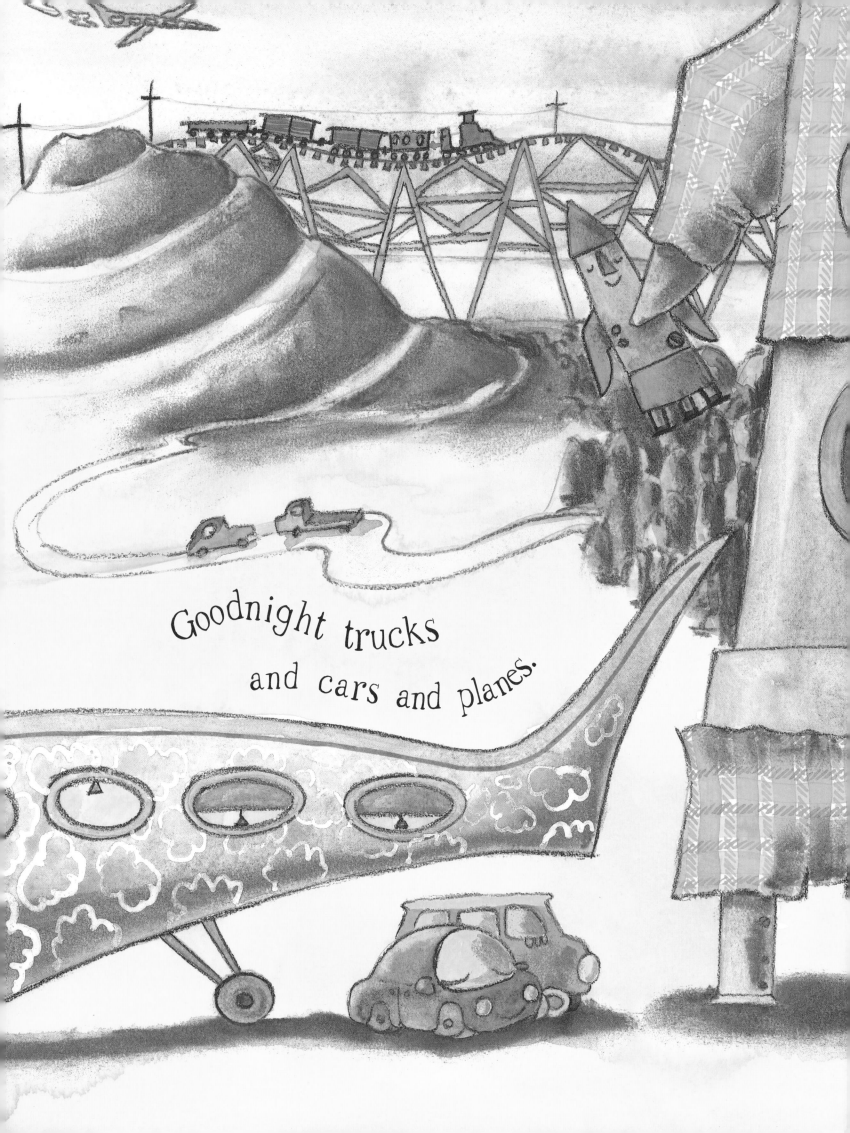

Goodnight trucks
and cars and planes.

Goodnight rockets,
goodnight trains.

Goodnight birds,
goodnight bees.

Goodnight fishes
in the seas.

Goodnight flowers,
goodnight grasses

curled up tight
while darkness passes.

Goodnight lions,
tigers, too,
and all the animals
in the zoo.

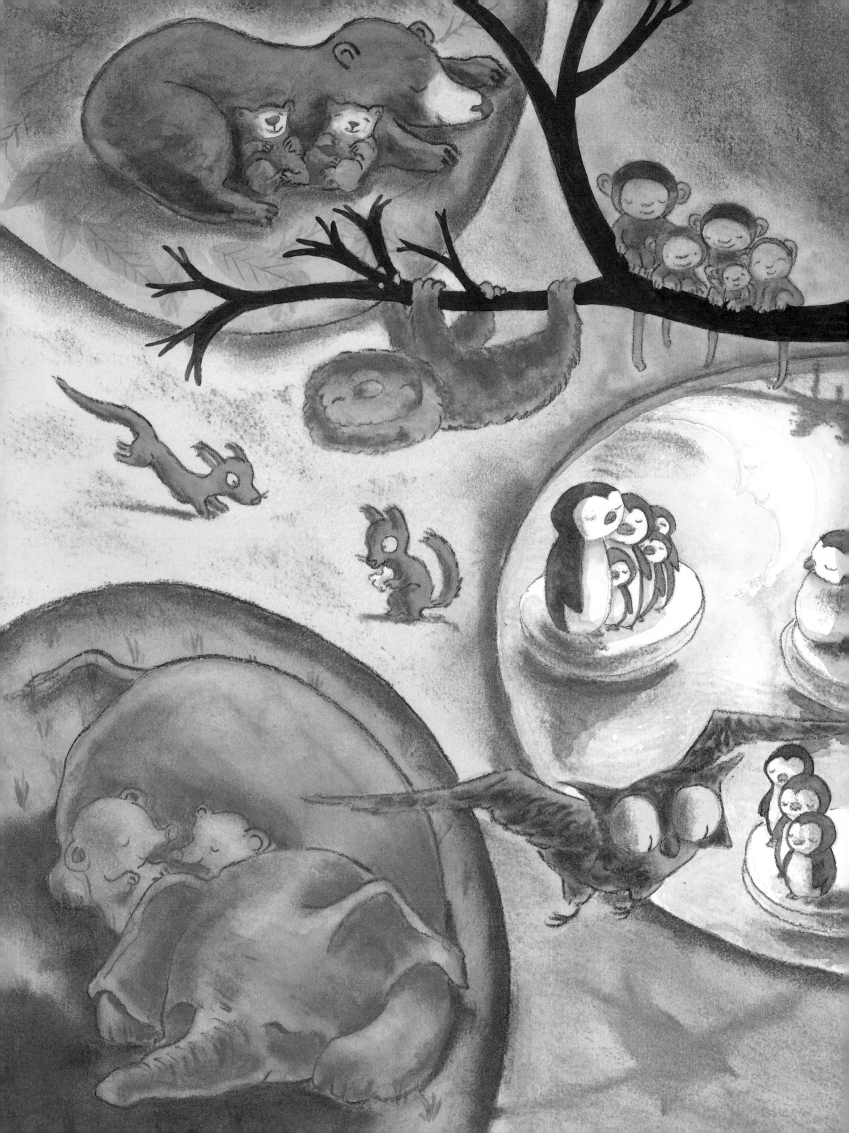

Goodnight shadows
in the park.

Goodnight dog
that doesn't bark.

Goodnight houses,
nests and burrows.

Goodnight daylight
until tomorrow's.

Goodnight teddies,
goodnight books.
Goodnight sparrows,
starlings, rooks.

Goodnight sounds
of distant cars,
and in the sky,
a million stars.

Goodnight moon,
Goodnight sun.
Goodnight, goodnight,
to everyone.

All is well
in my small world,

around my mother's heart
I'm curled.